# Marmaduke LAPS IT UP!

## BRAD ANDERSON

**TOR**

A TOM DOHERTY ASSOCIATES BOOK
NEW YORK

This is a work of fiction. All the characters and events portrayed in this book are fictional, and any resemblance to real people or incidents is purely coincidental.

**MARMADUKE LAPS IT UP!**

Copyright © 1986 by King Features Syndicate, Inc.

First printing: July 1989

A TOR Book

Published by Tom Doherty Associates, Inc.
49 West 24th Street
New York, N.Y. 10010

ISBN: 0-812-57335-8     Can. ISBN: 0-812-57336-6

Printed in the United States of America

0 9 8 7 6 5 4 3 2 1

Other Marmaduke titles
published by Tor Books

MARMADUKE HAMS IT UP!
MARMADUKE: I AM LOVABLE
MARMADUKE: IT'S A DOG'S LIFE
SITTING PRETTY, MARMADUKE

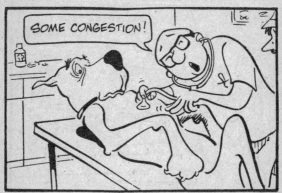

9-11

BRAD ANDERSON

SAY! I REALLY ENJOYED THE JOKES IN THIS MONTH'S **DOGS DIGEST**... PET PARADE WAS A LITTLE THIN... BUT **SPORTING DOGS** HAS SOME GOOD STORIES... AN' DO YOU SPOSE I COULD BORROW THE DOG HOUSE PLANS FROM THIS MONTH'S **MECHANIX**

... AN' YOU WON'T BELIEVE THIS LAST ONE!

9-18

IT LOOKS LIKE HE JOINED THE **BONE-OF-THE-MONTH CLUB!**

19

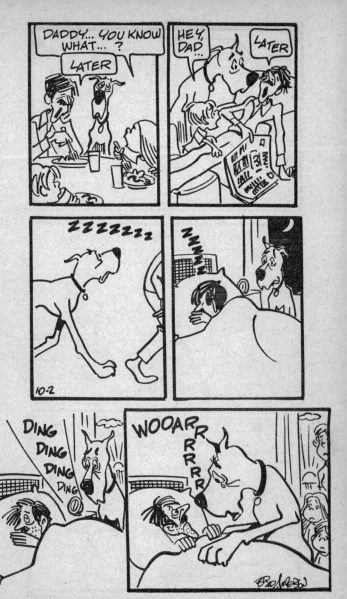

27

29

48

52

7-25

55

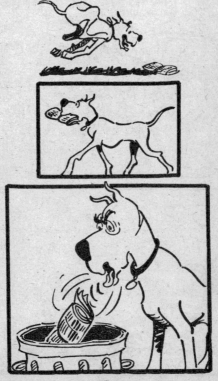

BRAD ANDERSON

61

69

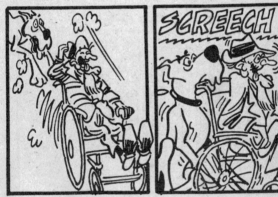

96

3-6

3-20

BRAD ANDERSON

117

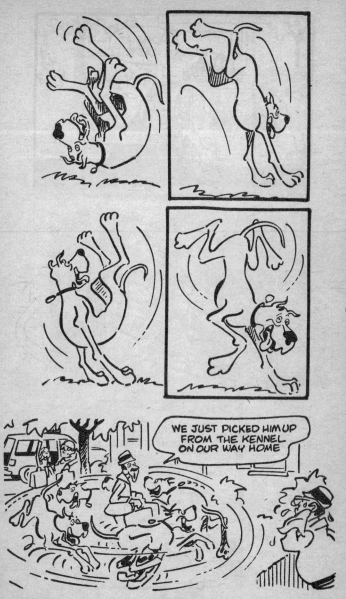

127